Dear Parents and Teachers,

In an easy-reader format, **My Readers** introduce classic stories to children who are learning to read. Favorite characters and time-tested tales are the basis for **My Readers**, which are available in three levels:

1 **Level One** is for the emergent reader and features repetitive language and word clues in the illustrations.

2 **Level Two** is for more advanced readers who still need support saying and understanding some words. Stories are longer with word clues in the illustrations.

3 **Level Three** is for independent, fluent readers who enjoy working out occasional unfamiliar words. The stories are longer and divided into chapters.

Encourage children to select books based on interests, not reading levels. Read aloud with children, showing them how to use the illustrations for clues. With adult guidance and rereading, children will eventually read the desired book on their own.

Here are some ways you might want to use this book with children:

- Talk about the title and the cover illustrations. Encourage the child to use these to predict what the story is about.
- Discuss the interior illustrations and try to piece together a story based on the pictures. Does the child want to change or adjust his first prediction?
- After children reread a story, suggest they retell or act out a favorite part.

My Readers will not only help children become readers, they will serve as an introduction to some of the finest classic children's books available today.

—LAURA ROBB
Educator and Reading Consultant

For activities and reading tips, visit myreadersonline.com.

For Mom and Dad
—K. D.

SQUARE
FISH

An Imprint of Macmillan Children's Publishing Group

RUDOLPH THE RED-NOSED REINDEER®. Rudolph the Red-Nosed Reindeer © & ® or
TM The Rudolph Co., L.P. All elements under license to Character Arts, LLC. All rights reserved.
Printed in China by Toppan Leefung Printing Ltd., Dongguan City, Guangdong Province.
For information, address Square Fish, 175 Fifth Avenue, New York, NY 10010.

Square Fish books may be purchased for business or promotional use. For information on bulk purchases,
please contact the Macmillan Corporate and Premium Sales Department at (800) 221-7945 x5442
or by e-mail at specialmarkets@macmillan.com

Library of Congress Cataloging-in-Publication Data Available

ISBN 978-1-250-05044-1 (hardcover)
1 3 5 7 9 10 8 6 4 2

ISBN 978-1-250-05048-9 (paperback)
1 3 5 7 9 10 8 6 4 2

Book design by Patrick Collins/Véronique Lefèvre Sweet

Square Fish logo designed by Filomena Tuosto

First MY READERS Edition: 2014

myreadersonline.com
mackids.com

This is a Level 2 book

Lexile 200L

RUDOLPH
THE
RED-NOSED
REINDEER®

Adapted by Kristen L. Depken
Cover illustrated by Artful Doodlers Ltd.
Interior illustrated by Linda Karl

SQUARE
FISH

Macmillan Children's Publishing Group
New York

Santa and his elves
lived in Christmastown.
They made toys
all year long.

One day,

a reindeer was born.

His name was Rudolph.

He had a red nose.

It glowed!

His parents were worried.
Rudolph's father
hid Rudolph's nose.

All the reindeer
wanted to pull
Santa's sled.
They were learning to fly.
Rudolph joined them.

Rudolph met Clarice.

She liked Rudolph.

Rudolph flew in the air!

The reindeer
cheered for Rudolph.
He was happy.

Rudolph's
fake nose fell off.
The reindeer laughed.
They called him Rudolph
the Red-Nosed Reindeer.

Poor Rudolph!

He ran away.

Hermey the elf
ran away, too.
He did not want
to make toys.
He wanted to be
a dentist.

Rudolph and Hermey
ran away together.
A snow monster began
to chase them!

A man named
Yukon Cornelius
helped them.

Yukon chopped the ice.
They floated away
from the monster.

They floated to an
island filled with toys.
These were toys
no one wanted.

The king of the island
wanted Rudolph to find
homes for the toys.
Rudolph knew
Santa would help.

The snow monster
could see Rudolph's nose.
Rudolph wanted to
protect his friends.

That night,

he left.

Rudolph went home.
His parents and Clarice
were missing!

The snow monster
had them!
Rudolph went
to the monster's cave.

Rudolph saved Clarice.

But the monster

grabbed him!

Yukon and Hermey

found Rudolph

just in time!

Hermey called
the snow monster.
Yukon dropped a rock
on the monster's head!

Everyone was safe!
They all went back
to Christmastown.

It was Christmas Eve!
But there was
a big storm.
Santa would have to
cancel Christmas!

Rudolph's nose

started to glow.

Santa got an idea.

Rudolph's nose
could light the way.

Christmas was saved!
Santa found homes
for all the toys.
And Rudolph
became the most
famous reindeer of all.